A GOLDEN JUNIOR GUIDE™

BUTTERFLIES
and MOTHS

By GEORGE S. FICHTER

Illustrated by KRISTIN KEST

Consultant: Dr. Norman Platnick, Curator,
Department of Entomology, American Museum of Natural History

A GOLDEN BOOK • NEW YORK
Western Publishing Company, Inc., Racine, Wisconsin 53404

Butterflies and Moths

are insects. More than a million kinds of insects have been identified. In fact, there are more insects in the world than any other kind of animal. Although insects come in many different sizes, shapes, and colors, most share these features:

- 2 *antennae,* or feelers
- 3 body parts:
  - head
  - thorax (midsection)
  - abdomen
- 6 legs
- 1 or 2 pairs of wings

Butterflies and Moths use their tubelike tongue, or *proboscis,* to suck up liquids.

tongue

A Butterfly or Moth keeps its tongue coiled up when it isn't eating.

Promethea Moth

tongue

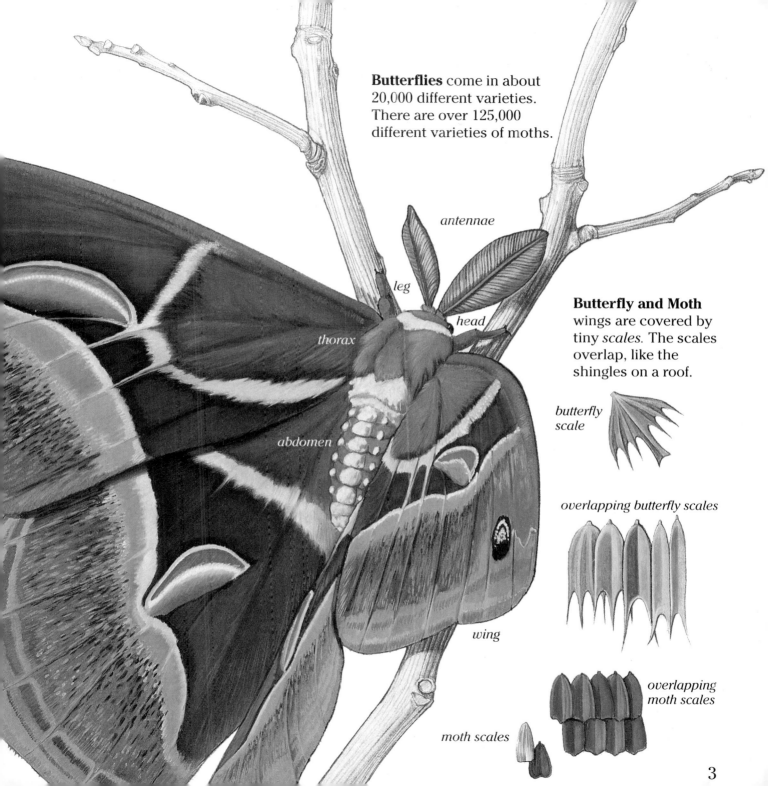

Butterflies come in about 20,000 different varieties. There are over 125,000 different varieties of moths.

antennae

leg

head

thorax

abdomen

Butterfly and Moth wings are covered by tiny *scales*. The scales overlap, like the shingles on a roof.

butterfly scale

overlapping butterfly scales

wing

overlapping moth scales

moth scales

3

Can You Tell Which Is Which?

In the following pages, you will meet some of the most commonly seen or familiar butterflies and moths. Butterflies and moths are not always easy to tell apart. But you should be able to spot some of the differences between them.

Moths

- ☐ Most moths have a thick body covered with hair.
- ☐ Moth colors are often dull and drab.
- ☐ Moth antennae are either slim or feathery.
- ☐ Most moths fly at night or in dim light.

Satin Moth

White Underwing Moth

Imperial Moth

types of moth antennae

A Moth at rest holds its wings, like a little roof, over its body. Or, it may spread its wings out flat.

Butterflies
- ☐ Butterflies have a slim body that has no hair.
- ☐ Butterfly colors are usually bright.
- ☐ Butterfly antennae are slim and have "knobs" on the ends.
- ☐ Butterflies fly during the daylight.

Buckeye Butterfly

A Butterfly at rest holds its wings straight up.

knobs on butterfly antennae

5

How Big? How Small?

Butterflies and moths come in many different sizes. How do we measure a butterfly or a moth? One way is by measuring its *wingspan*. This is the distance from the tip of one open wing (or pair of wings) to the tip of the other.

The Two-tailed Swallowtail Butterfly has a wingspan of up to 6 inches. It is one of the largest butterflies in North America.

(Note: Insects pictured in this book may be larger than actual size, to show more detail.)

Two-tailed Swallowtail Butterfly

Pygmy Blue Butterfly

The Pygmy Blue is one of the smallest butterflies. Its wings span about half an inch. It would take more than 250 tiny Pygmy Blues to cover these two pages.

Cecropia Moth

*Solitary Oak Leaf
Miner Moth*

The Cecropia Moth
has wings that span
more than 6 inches.
It is one of the
largest moths in
North America.

The Solitary Oak Leaf Miner Moth
has wings that span less than a
quarter of an inch. It is one of the
smallest moths in the world.

Did You Know?

The biggest butterflies
and moths live in the
tropics. They can have a
wingspan of more than
11 inches. This is roughly
the size of a football.

Butterflies and Moths Begin

life as eggs that hatch into tiny caterpillars. The female butterfly or moth lays her eggs on or near a plant. This plant will serve as food for the caterpillars when they hatch. With their powerful jaws, the baby caterpillars munch nonstop. They are like little machines. They eat and eat, growing bigger every day.

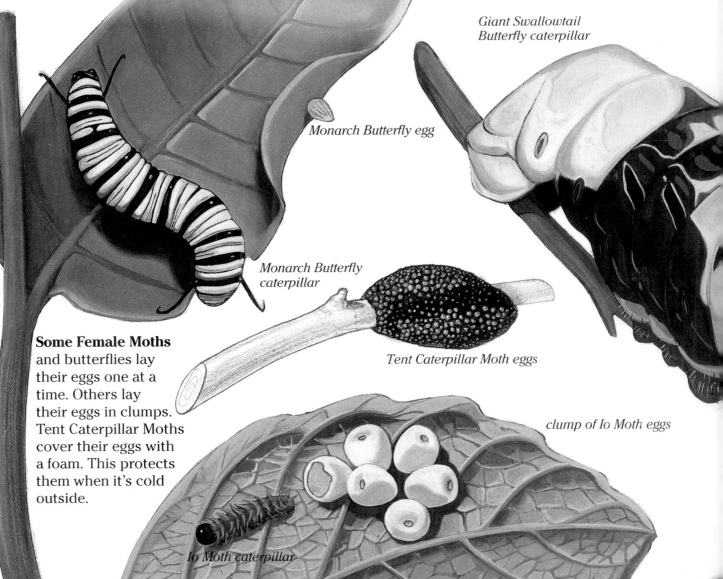

Giant Swallowtail Butterfly caterpillar

Monarch Butterfly egg

Monarch Butterfly caterpillar

Tent Caterpillar Moth eggs

clump of Io Moth eggs

Some Female Moths and butterflies lay their eggs one at a time. Others lay their eggs in clumps. Tent Caterpillar Moths cover their eggs with a foam. This protects them when it's cold outside.

Io Moth caterpillar

8

Some Caterpillars, such as the Saddleback Moth caterpillar, are covered with stiff hairs or spines. These can sting! Birds and other predators usually leave these caterpillars alone.

Saddleback caterpillar

Did You Know?

When a caterpillar grows too big for its skin, the skin splits. The caterpillar then crawls out, wearing a new, stretchy skin. This *shedding* happens several times before a caterpillar is fully grown.

9

A Big Change

occurs when a caterpillar reaches its full size. It stops feeding, sheds its skin again, and becomes a *pupa*. Even though this stage of its life is sometimes called the resting stage, a lot is going on. The wormlike creature is changing into a delicate, beautiful adult with wings!

Many Insects spend their pupal stage inside a protective covering known as a *cocoon*. The cocoon of a butterfly is called a *chrysalis*. This is the chrysalis of a Monarch Butterfly.

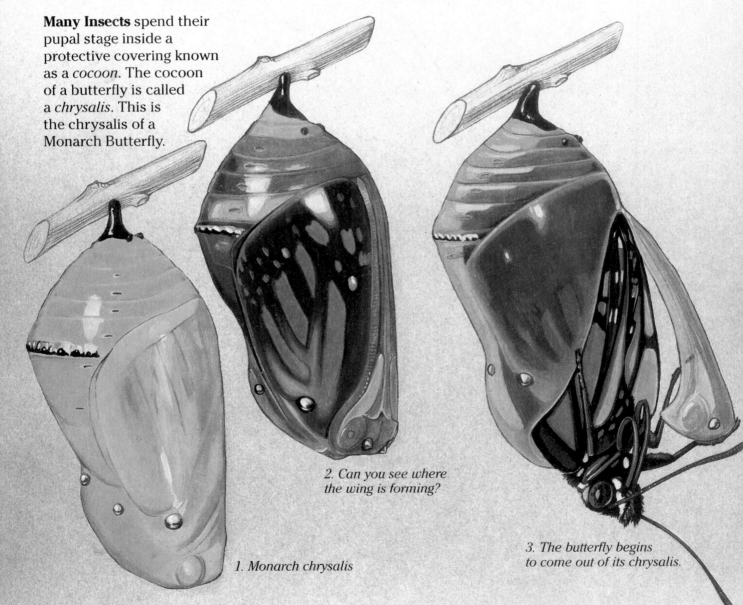

1. Monarch chrysalis

2. Can you see where the wing is forming?

3. The butterfly begins to come out of its chrysalis.

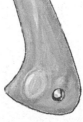

A Butterfly emerges from its chrysalis with its tongue in two halves. Until these halves permanently join a short while later, the butterfly cannot suck up liquids.

4. When a butterfly or moth emerges, its wings are small, wrinkled, and limp. They fill with fluid and straighten out. Then they harden.

5. The adult Monarch Butterfly takes to the air.

Monarch Butterflies can fly fast and far. In fact, they are champion fliers! In fall, great flocks of them head for warmer climates. They may travel 80 miles or more every day. Some Monarchs that live in Canada fly as far south as Mexico.

Monarchs stop to rest on the same bushes or trees year after year. If a long-used stopping place has been destroyed, hundreds of the butterflies will swarm around where it used to be. Amazingly, this happens even if none of them has ever made the trip before.

Did You Know?

Monarchs can fly at speeds of up to 20 miles per hour. That's a lot faster than you can ride your bike! Monarchs also taste and smell bad. This helps protect them from being eaten by predators.

Viceroy Butterflies

look a lot like Monarchs. A bird that has learned not to eat Monarchs will probably stay away from Viceroys, too! In fact, many insects that are brightly colored, such as Viceroys and Monarchs, are actually warning others that eating them will be a very distasteful–or even dangerous– experience. Viceroys like to fly in wide-open spaces, such as meadows and roadsides. They fly even faster than Monarchs.

Monarch Butterfly

Monarchs and Viceroys look quite similar. But the Viceroy is smaller. Also, do you see the extra black line on the wings of the Viceroy? Does the Monarch have this same line?

black line

Viceroy Butterfly

Viceroy Butterflies, like other butterflies, smell and taste with their feet!

Viceroys glide with wings held out to the sides. Monarchs hold their wings upright when gliding.

Viceroy caterpillars look just like bird droppings to many other animals. This protects the caterpillars from predators.

caterpillar

chrysalis

15

Fritillaries

Fritillaries belong to a large group called *Brush-footed Butterflies*. On their tiny front legs are clumps of bristles. These are useless for walking or for holding on to things. Instead, the bristles are used like brushes, to clean the insect's antennae.

The Fritillary caterpillar has spines on its skin. These have small "branches" coming out of them. The Fritillary's chrysalis is covered with bumps.

chrysalis

Great Spangled Fritillary

Great Spangled Fritillary caterpillar

This Fritillary has large silver spots on the undersides of its wings. These make it easy to identify the butterfly.

front legs, with brushes

female Diana Fritillary

Did You Know?
Male and Female Dianas
are different colors.

Diana Fritillaries love
woods and thickets.

Did You Also Know?
Dianas are not usually
attracted to flowers. However,
like some other species, they
are drawn to manure piles.

male Diana Fritillary

Swallowtails

get their name from the birdlike "tails" that usually stick out from behind their back wings. Most Swallowtail Butterflies have only one tail on each wing. But some have two or three tails. Others have none. Swallowtails are the biggest butterflies in the United States.

Tiger Swallowtail caterpillar

male Spicebush Swallowtail

"horns"

Swallowtail caterpillars, when disturbed, display yellow or orange "horns" on their head. These give off a strong, unpleasant odor.

*Eastern Tiger
Swallowtail Butterfly*

tails

female Spicebush Swallowtail

*Spicebush
caterpillar*

Some Swallowtail caterpillars rest in a
leaf that they have folded over with silk.

Alfalfa and Cabbage Butterflies are very common

and easy to find. They are among the first butterflies to appear in the spring. They are the last to be seen in fall. Caterpillars of these species are often considered pests because they eat valuable food crops. Look for the butterflies along the side of a road, in your own backyard, in a garden, or in a field.

male

Alfalfa Butterflies

female

20

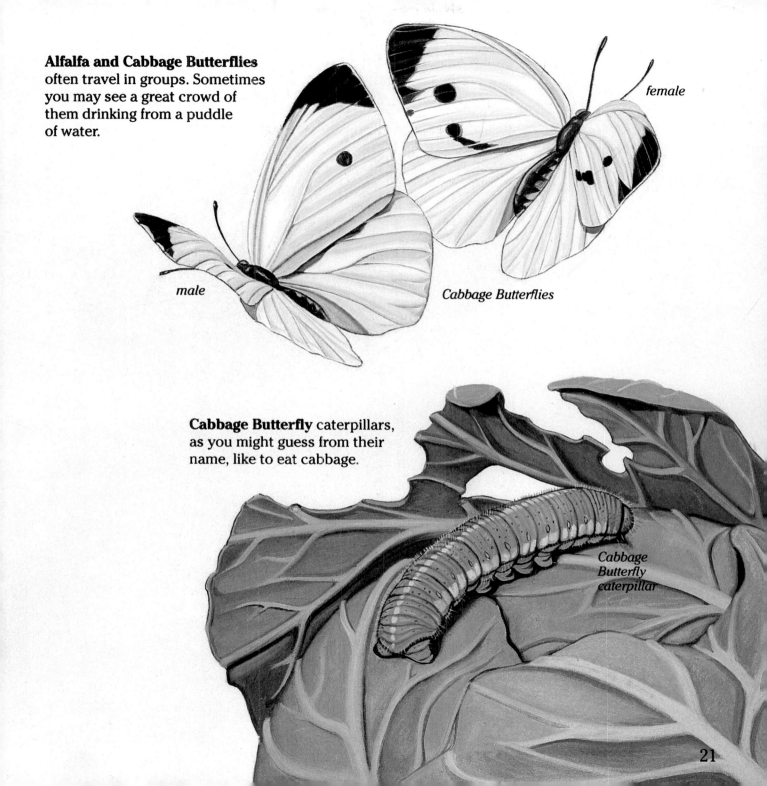

Alfalfa and Cabbage Butterflies often travel in groups. Sometimes you may see a great crowd of them drinking from a puddle of water.

female

male

Cabbage Butterflies

Cabbage Butterfly caterpillars, as you might guess from their name, like to eat cabbage.

Cabbage Butterfly caterpillar

21

Painted Ladies are butterflies you might see anywhere in the world. They sometimes travel in *swarms,* or large groups, in search of food. They especially like thistles. They can cross big lakes and sometimes have been seen far out at sea.

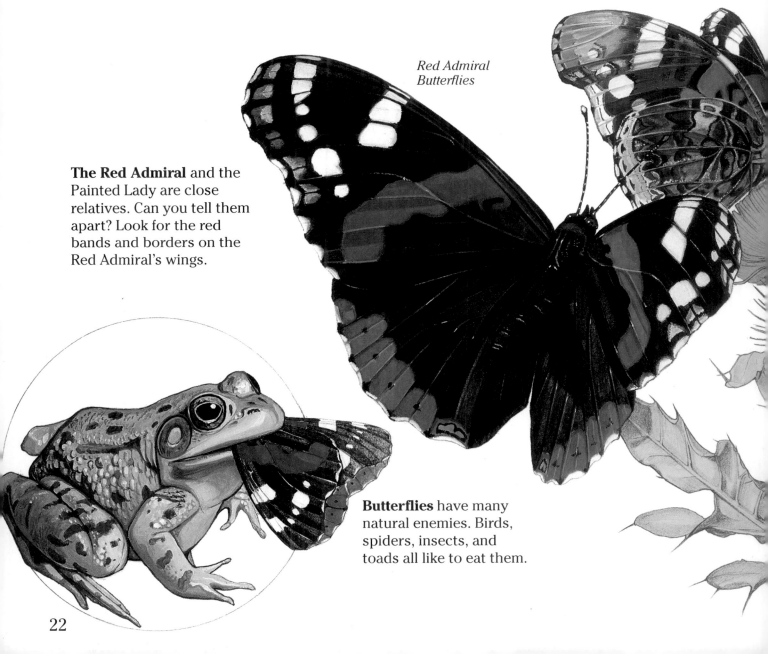

Red Admiral Butterflies

The Red Admiral and the Painted Lady are close relatives. Can you tell them apart? Look for the red bands and borders on the Red Admiral's wings.

Butterflies have many natural enemies. Birds, spiders, insects, and toads all like to eat them.

Painted Lady Butterfly

Painted Ladies, like most butterflies, have wings that are one color and pattern on the top and a different color and pattern on the underside!

top of wing

underside of wing

Painted Lady caterpillar

chrysalis

23

Sphinx Moths

are also called *Hawkmoths* because of their swift flight. Some can fly up to 35 miles an hour. That's ten times faster than you could walk, even if you hurried! These moths unroll their long tongues to suck the sweet fluid, called *nectar,* from flowers. You may see them feeding in the evening. Petunia nectar is one of their favorite foods.

Achemon Sphinx Moth

The Achemon Sphinx is one of the more colorful moths in this group.

Most Sphinx Moth pupae are found in loose soil. The loop at the front of the pupa is where the moth's tongue is growing.

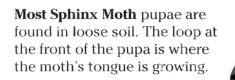

Tomato Hornworm

Five-spotted Hawkmoth

The Five-spotted Hawkmoth caterpillar is also called the Tomato Hornworm because it is a common garden pest. Here it holds up its body in a fierce-looking pose. This scares off birds and other predators.

25

Hummingbird and Bumblebee Moths are two kinds of
Sphinx Moths. You might spot either during the day. They both feed on the nectar of
flowers. Most moths stand on flowers to feed. But some feed while hovering in the
air, with their long tongues outstretched.

Did You Know?
Not all butterflies and
moths drink nectar
from flowers. Some
drink sap from trees.

**The Hummingbird
Moth's** tongue is
longer than its
whole body!

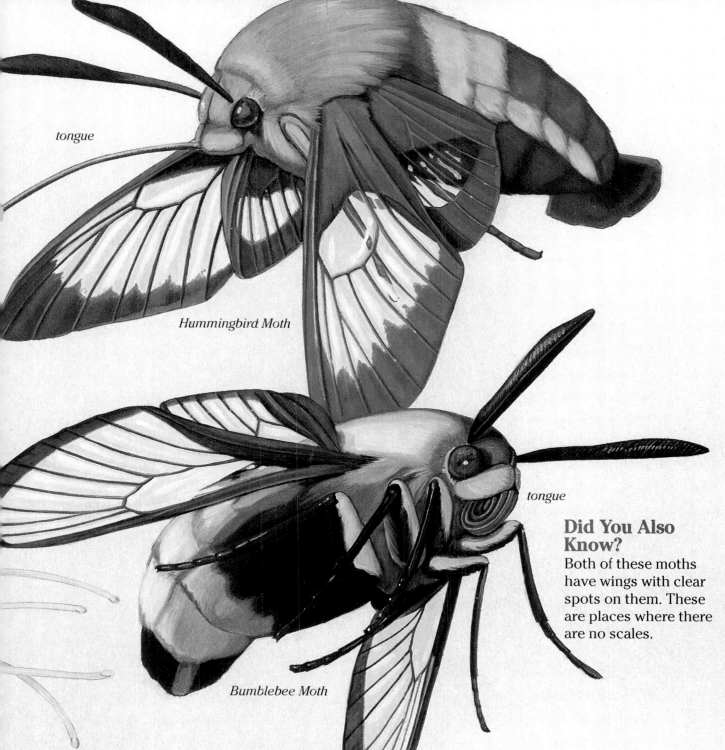

tongue

Hummingbird Moth

tongue

Did You Also Know?

Both of these moths have wings with clear spots on them. These are places where there are no scales.

Bumblebee Moth

Isabella Moths belong to a group of insects called *Tiger Moths*. This is because of the stripes and spots on their wings. Isabella Moth caterpillars are called *Woolly Bears*. There is an old saying that a lot of black hair at the front and rear of the caterpillar's body means the coming winter will be very cold. However, scientists have found no evidence for this.

Woolly Bear

Woolly Bears mix their own hairs with silk to make their cocoons.

Isabella Moth

Great Leopard Moth

Virgo Tiger Moth

The Tiger Moth group includes all of these moths.

Bella Moth

Bats eat lots of night-flying moths. But some moths have ways to escape the bats. Tiger Moths, for example, taste bad. They also make clicking sounds they hope will scare bats away.

Luna Moths

are very beautiful. They are greenish white with clear "windows" on their wings and long, curved tails. The front wings are bordered with purple in spring, more brownish in fall. Luna Moths fly mainly at night. You are most likely to see them on warm evenings in wooded areas.

face

male Luna Moth

The Male Luna Moth's antennae are larger and more feathery than the female's. The male's sensitive antennae can pick up the scent of a female 5 miles away!

cocoon

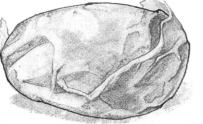

A Luna Moth caterpillar spins a silken cocoon. The outside of the cocoon looks like paper. But it is very tough.

The Polyphemus Moth is a relative of the Luna Moth. See the big eyespots on its hind wings? These fake eyes scare off most predators.

Polyphemus Moth

Polyphemus Moth caterpillar

Black Witches belong to a group of insects that are sometimes called *Owlet Moths*. This is because, like owls, they fly at night. Their eyes "glow" in the dark when light shines on them. Black Witches are the giants among Owlet Moths. They have a wingspan of up to 6 inches. Other Owlet Moths are smaller. You are most likely to see Black Witch Moths in warm climates, but they sometimes stray as far north as Canada.

Black Witch Moth

Armyworm Moth

Underwing Moth flying

Armyworm Moths belong to the same group as the Black Witch. The caterpillars travel in large numbers, or "armies," as they search for food. They travel at night and hide during the day.

Underwing Moths are Owlet Moths, too. They have brightly colored hind wings that show only when the moths fly. Predators can't see them when they land on trees because, with their hind wings covered, they look just like tree bark!

Armyworm Moth caterpillars

Underwing Moth resting

33

Bagworm Moths come from eggs that hatch into caterpillars.
The caterpillars immediately spin silken sacs, or "bags," around themselves.
Look for these "bags" in evergreen trees and shrubs. Only the head and front part
of the caterpillar's body stick out as the caterpillar feeds on the plant's leaves.

*larva
feeding*

*male
Bagworm
Moth*

*bagworm sac,
covered with
needles,
hanging
from tree*

Did You Know?
A female Bagworm Moth doesn't
develop legs or wings. She spends
almost all of her life inside the bag
where she was born!

Male Bagworm Moths emerge as tiny, nearly clear-winged creatures. They quickly fly off in search of mates.

male pupa

female pupa

Bagworm Moth caterpillars stay in their bags for the pupal stage.

35

For Further Reading

With this book, you've only just begun to explore some exciting new worlds. Why not continue to learn about the insects known as butterflies and moths? For example, you might want to browse through *Butterflies and Moths (Golden Guide),* which contains many fascinating details on the insects in this book and additional ones as well. Also, be sure to visit your local library, where you will discover a variety of titles on the subject. Two other Golden Books you might enjoy are: *I Wonder Where Butterflies Go in Winter and Other Neat Facts About Insects* and *The Golden Book of Insects and Spiders.*